W9-ANP-791

Our Friendship Rules

Peggy Moss and Dee Dee Tardif

Illustrated by
Alissa Imre Geis

TILBURY HOUSE, PUBLISHERS ❧ GARDINER, MAINE

When my friend Jenny Martin hides, she is almost impossible to find.

Unless she starts talking.

Jenny Martin is my best friend.

We sit next to each other on the bus.

We play cards in her tree house.

We spy on my brother.

During recess, we play "Jenny Tag."

It's really complicated.
And fun.

We made up rules.
Jenny keeps them in her pocket,

just in case.

the
official
Jenny
tag
rules

I have a lot of pictures of my friend Jenny.
This one is my favorite:

This is my next favorite picture
of Jenny:

1st

2nd

(Jenny promised that next time she makes a puppet
out of one of my best shirts, she'll ask first.)

Rolinda Sparks moved to our school recently.
Here is a picture of Rolinda Sparks:

Rolinda Sparks

Rolinda Sparks is absolutely the coolest
kid I've ever seen.

The moment I saw Rolinda Sparks,
I wanted her to be my friend.
I bet you would want that, too.

Rolinda's shoes

So I came up with a plan.

I found a pair of shoes just like Rolinda's in my sister's closet.

I stuffed tissue in the toes.

And I wore them to school.

At morning recess I couldn't play jump rope because I kept tripping over the pointy tips.

But when Rolinda Sparks noticed my shoes at lunch, she smiled.

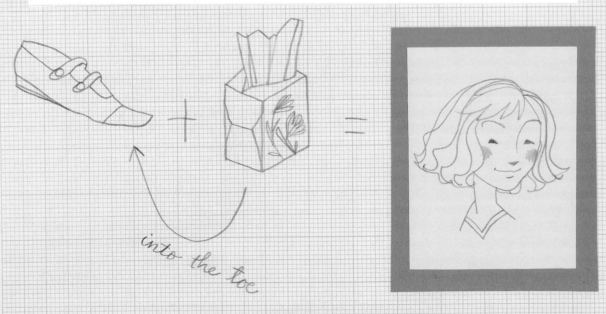

into the toe

Then, I cut my hair just like Rolinda's, and the most amazing thing happened.

Rolinda Sparks said I could be her friend.

Can you believe it?

Rolinda sat next to me on the way to the science museum field trip.

She said there wasn't enough room for Jenny.

Rolinda let me sit at her table at lunch.

She and her friends talked about how Jenny Martin looks just like a lizard because she is so small.

"All she does is run around and hide under things," Rolinda laughed.

I sat quiet as a leaf. I didn't say a word.

Rolinda looked at me. "You aren't still friends with her, are you?"

I wanted Rolinda to be my friend.   So I lied.
(I bet you would have done the same thing if you were me.)

"Jenny and I aren't really friends anymore," I said. "She talks too loud."

I felt a little sick to my stomach when I said it. But only for a minute, because Rolinda smiled a big welcome-to-my-club smile and said, "You're right!"

I felt so good, so fabulously clever, that I said, "I know tons of secrets about Jenny."

Rolinda beamed. I beamed back.

And then I told one of Jenny's biggest, most private secrets, one that I'd sworn never to tell.

When Jenny found out that I told her secret,
she got really, really mad.

This is what Jenny Martin
looks like when she is mad.

This is what Jenny Martin looks like when she is hurt.

And this is what Jenny Martin looks like when she can't believe that her best friend told a story about her

just to impress
the coolest girl in the school.

BY AIR MAIL
PAR AVION

unkindly

betrayed

pained

wickedness

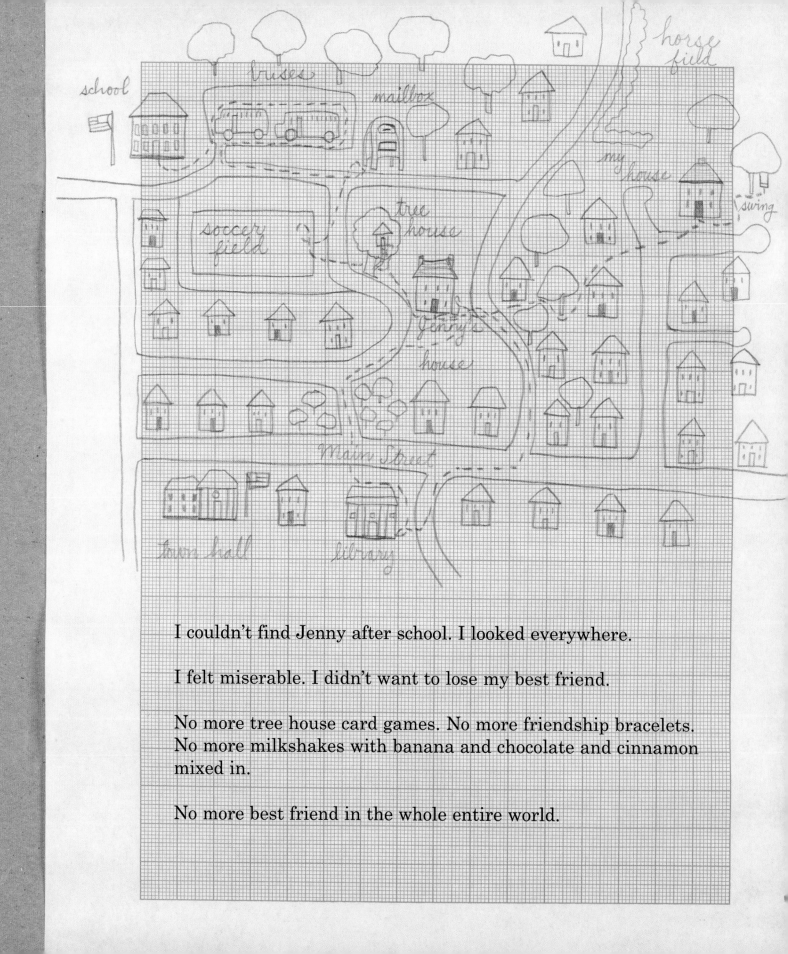

I couldn't find Jenny after school. I looked everywhere.

I felt miserable. I didn't want to lose my best friend.

No more tree house card games. No more friendship bracelets. No more milkshakes with banana and chocolate and cinnamon mixed in.

No more best friend in the whole entire world.

"I'm sorry," I said.

This is what Jenny Martin said from her hiding place. "You should be sorry. You thought telling my secret would make you look cool?"

"Sometimes I'm not so smart," I said.

"Right," Jenny said.

She didn't say anything else for a long time.

I thought about the times we'd gotten into fights before. We always worked things out, even if we had to cry first.

But this felt different. Worse.

"I'm really, really sorry," I said.

Jenny climbed out of her hiding place. She had a crinkled-up piece of paper in her hand. "Remember this?" she asked.

I remembered.

Jenny and Alexandra's Friendship Rules

1. Never make a puppet out of your friend's clothes without asking.
2. It's okay to get mad at your friend. It is okay to shout. It is okay to cry. It is <u>not</u> okay to throw milkshake at her.
3. IMPORTANT: It is easier to find a new favorite shirt than a new best friend.

In a quiet voice, Jenny said, "I think we need to add some more rules."

We worked all afternoon. Sometimes we laughed.
Sometimes we didn't.
But finally we had a whole bunch of friendship rules.

Just in case there's ever another
Rolinda Sparks.

Jenny and Alexandra's
New Friendship Rules

When we finished writing down our rules,
I took the wrinkled-up piece of paper
home and copied every word onto
a fresh piece of paper.

Then I put our friendship rules in my
pocket, just in case.

I don't spend much time with Rolinda Sparks. I don't try to look like her, either.

(This is a pretty good picture of me.)

The other day, Rolinda Sparks asked if she could play jump rope with us.

"Sure," I said. "Our rules say anybody can play."

Guess what? Rolinda Sparks likes that rule a lot.

TILBURY HOUSE, PUBLISHERS
103 Brunswick Avenue, Gardiner, Maine 04345
800-582-1899 · www.tilburyhouse.com

Text copyright © 2007 by Margaret Paula Moss and Madeline Paula Moss Tardif
Illustrations copyright © 2007 by Alissa Imre Geis
All rights reserved.

First hardcover printing: May 2007 · 10 9 8 7 6 5 4 3 2
First paperback printing: June 2011 · 10 9 8 7 6 5 4 3 2 1

For Emily and Anna. Thanks to Dee Dee for the inspiration, Audrey and Jennifer
for their patience, and my sisters, by blood and love, for showing me
the best that friendship can offer. —PM

To my brothers, Charlie and Daniel, and my cousins, the best friends of all.
Thanks to Peggy for the opportunity; my aunts, uncles, and grandparents for
their boatloads of love; and Mom and Dad, for everything. —DT

For Stacey. —AIG

Library of Congress Cataloging-in-Publication Data

Moss, Peggy, 1966-
Our friendship rules / Peggy Moss and Dee Dee Tardif ;
illustrated by Alissa Imre Geis.
        p. cm.
Summary: Alexandra tells one of her best friend Jenny's most important secrets
in an effort to be accepted by a cool new girl at school, and then she must try to
rescue her friendship with Jenny.
ISBN 978-0-88448-291-8 (hard cover : alk. paper)
[1. Best friends—Fiction. 2. Friendship—Fiction. 3. Peer pressure—Fiction. 4.
Children's writings.] I. Tardif, Dee Dee, 1992- II. Geis, Alissa Imre, ill. III. Title.
PZ7.M85357Ou 2007
[E]—dc22   2006037837

Designed by Geraldine Millham, Westport, Massachusetts
Editing and production: Audrey Maynard, Karen Fisk, Jennifer Bunting
Printed and bound by: Sung In Printing Ltd., Dang Jung-Dong 242-2, GungPo-si,
Kyunggi-do, Korea; June 2011